He's Your Dog!

Library of Congress catalog card number: 93-10095
Published simultaneously in Canada by HarperCollins*CanadaLtd*
Color separations by Hong Kong Scanner Craft
Printed and bound in the United States of America
by Berryville Graphics
Designed by Martha Rago
First edition, 1993

He's Your Dog!

PAT SCHORIES

Farrar · Straus · Giroux

New York

NORTH END

Maybe we'll go down South, and live on the beach. We'll eat ice cream and camp out at night. But what if it rains? We'd have no place to sleep.

I know, we'll go to an all-night truck stop and sleep in the kitchen.

Only, what if they don't allow dogs?

kay, so we'll hitchhike. A truck driver with one of those sleeping shelves in his cab will pick us up. But you, you won't have any place to run.

aybe some rich lady with a chauffeur will come along instead. I'll say I'm an orphan, and she can adopt us.

But what about my best friend, Tony?

I know! We'll build a tree house in the big oak, and Tony can help. He'll sneak us tools and wood from his garage.

ey, maybe we should just move into Tony's garage. There's all that stuff up in the loft.

And we can spy on our house.

Except there's a ladder. And you can't climb.

How about moving into the doghouse? There's plenty of room. And if Mom ever tries to get rid of you, she'll have to get rid of me, too.

ut what if she really does
try to get rid of you? I
won't let her. I'll stay
right here in the closet and watch her every move.

I'll give you obedience lessons.
Mom will be amazed! I'll teach
you to sit! Beg! Roll over!

And to never, never…

ever chew shoes!

nd I know she will let you stay.